Margaret Miller

CAN YOU GUESS?

Greenwillow Books, New York

I want to thank all the children in this book for happily sharing so many
playful moments with me: Miranda Berman, Jamie Cornwall, Alexi Greenberg,
Kenya Harris, Jason Joung, Justin Kruger, Alexandra Rodriguez,
Randy Shorter, and Marissa Solomon.

The full-color photographs were reproduced from 35-mm Kodachrome 25 slides.
The text type is Avant Garde Gothic Medium and Demi Bold.

Printed in Singapore by Tien Wah Press
First Edition   10 9 8 7 6 5 4 3 2 1

Library of Congress Cataloging-in-Publication Data
Miller, Margaret (date)
Can you guess? / by Margaret Miller.
p.   cm.
Summary: Suggests both right and wrong answers
to such questions as "What do you give to your dog?"
and "What do you wear to bed?"
ISBN 0-688-11180-7 (trade).   ISBN 0-688-11181-5 (lib. bdg.)
[1. Vocabulary — Fiction.
2. Questions and answers — Fiction.]
I. Title.   PZ7.M628Can   1993
[E] — dc20   92-29406   CIP   AC

For David,
my sweetie

What do you comb in the morning?

A blouse?

Your face?

Your leg?

A bar of soap?

Your hair!

What do you give to your dog?

A dress?

A book?

Sunglasses?

A phone?

A dog biscuit!

What do you pack in a suitcase?

Three bears?

Yourself?

A pumpkin?

Two dogs?

Clothes!

What do you send in the mail?

A basketball?

An elephant?

The ocean?

A watermelon?

A letter!

What
do you
put
on
your
head?

A cloud?

An
ice cream
sundae?

Underpants?

A lunchbox?

A hat!

What do you plant in the ground?

A roller skate?

A mitten?

Eggs?

Your foot?

Flowers!

What do you eat for dinner?

Blocks?

A football?

A shoe?

Hay?

Spaghetti!

What do you wash in the sink?

A pizza?

A birthday present?

Newspaper?

Cows?

Dishes!

What do you wear to bed?

A cardboard box?

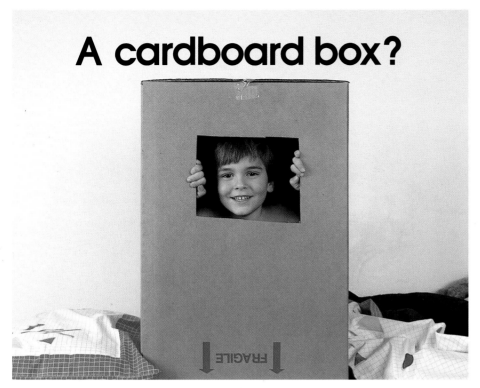

Boots?

Skis?

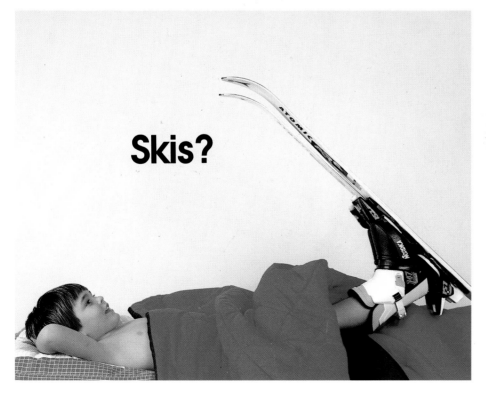

Aluminum foil?

Pajamas!

MARGARET MILLER is a freelance photographer who lives in New York City with her husband, two children, and three dogs. She traces her love of photography to her childhood. "My mother is a wonderful photographer and I grew up in a house filled with family photographs. I especially loved being with her in the darkroom. I also spent many hours looking through two very powerful books, *The Family of Man* edited by Edward Steichen, and *You Have Seen Their Faces* by Erskine Caldwell and Margaret Bourke-White. After college I worked in children's book publishing for a number of years. I had always taken photographs of my family and I was fortunate in realizing my goal of combining my two long-time interests—photography and children's books."

Margaret Miller is the author/photographer of *Whose Hat?, Who Uses This?, Whose Shoe?,* and *Where Does It Go?,* a *New York Times* Best Illustrated Book of 1992. She is also the photographer for *Ramona: Behind the Scenes of a Television Show; Safe in the Spotlight; Funny Papers; The President Builds a House; Your New Potty; My Puppy Is Born;* and *How You Were Born.*